POP HOOPER'S
PERFECT PETS

Funny
Little
Dog

D0895971

POP HOOPER'S
PERFECT PETS

Funny Little Dog

KYLE MEWBURN

ILLUSTRATED BY **HEATH MCKENZIE**

LITTLE 🐇 HARE
www.littleharebooks.com

Little Hare Books
an imprint of
Hardie Grant Egmont
85 High Street
Prahran, Victoria, 3181, Australia

www.littleharebooks.com

First published 2009
Reprinted 2011

National Library of Australia
Cataloguing-in-Publication entry

Mewburn, Kyle, 1963-

Funny little dog / Kyle Mewburn ; illustrator, Heath McKenzie

978 1 921272 76 9 (pbk.)

Pop Hooper's perfect pets ; 2

For primary school age.

Dogs—Juvenile fiction

McKenzie, Heath.

NZ823.2

Cover design by Natalie Winter
Set in 13.5/24.5 pt Stone Informal by Clinton Ellicott
Printed by WKT Company Limited
Printed in Shenzhen, Guangdong Province, China, February 2011

6 5 4 3 2

This product conforms to CPSIA 2008

One

Flyn hung upside down from the oak tree, with his limbs wrapped tightly around a branch. He held his breath and carefully turned his head so he could scan the park. The boys were standing directly below him. Flyn could have dropped an acorn down Toby Downer's collar. But that was the *last* thing Flyn wanted to do.

1

He just wanted to get to school without a fight.

Toby Downer had a sixth sense for finding Flyn. 'The little chicken's got to be around here somewhere. If he hasn't done that assignment for me, he's mincemeat,' he said.

'Yeah!' Brad and Jason Dimble snorted. They agreed with everything Toby Downer said.

Flyn gritted his teeth and tried to heave himself silently back onto the branch. He'd still be sitting there safely if that stupid caterpillar hadn't crawled over his hand and frightened him into losing his balance.

The branch creaked.

CREEAAK!!

'What was that?' Toby Downer hissed.

Flyn tried to gulp, but his mouth was dry. Toby Downer was bound to see him.

'Let's split up!' Toby Downer suddenly barked. 'The chicken's got to show his ugly face sometime.'

Flyn watched
as Brad Dimble
ducked into a
hedge near the
park entrance,
cutting off Flyn's
path back to the
main road, and his
easiest route to school.
Jason Dimble doubled
back towards Flyn's house,
then hid behind a wheelie bin,
in case Flyn tried to sneak home.
And Toby Downer ...

Flyn craned his neck in both
directions. There was no sign of Toby
Downer. He could have hidden
anywhere!

4

Flyn's only hope was to catch them off guard. If he could make it across the river with a head start, he might be able to outrun them. There was a cycle path curling around the back of Lookout Hill that would bring him out onto the main road at the opposite end of town. It was a long way and he would be late for school. But that would be better than facing Toby Downer's gang now.

Flyn arched his back and peered through the branches.

The Dimbles were already bored.
They were hardly watching any more.
Flyn could see Jason Dimble behind
the wheelie bin across the park.
He was scratching the gutter with a
rock. Brad Dimble was busy breaking
twigs off the hedge.

If only Flyn knew where Toby
Downer was hiding.

Flyn took three deep breaths, then
clambered out of the tree as fast as he
could. He hit the ground running.

'There he is!' yelled Brad Dimble.

'Get him!' Jason Dimble called.

Flyn didn't glance back. He leapt
over a flowerbed and cut across the
park towards the river. When he saw
the bridge, he sighed with relief.

The bridge was the perfect place for an ambush. It was only wide enough for one person to cross at a time. But Toby Downer was nowhere to be seen.

The bridge swayed and rumbled as Flyn sprinted across it.

'Don't let him get away!' Brad Dimble called.

Then Jason Dimble cheered: 'Get him, Toby!'

Toby Downer sprang out from behind a bulldozer parked on the opposite riverbank and ran to cut Flyn off. Flyn gritted his teeth and charged. There was no way he was going to let Toby Downer trap him on the bridge.

A metre from the end of the bridge, Flyn leapt at Toby Downer. Growling angrily, Toby Downer lunged towards him. Flyn was sure they would collide. But then Toby Downer flinched, and Flyn shot past him. Toby Downer clutched at Flyn's backpack, missed, and sprawled forwards onto the gravel track.

As Flyn tried to jump clear, Toby Downer threw out a hand. It clipped Flyn's ankle, knocking him off balance. Instead of heading left towards the cycle path and safety, Flyn stumbled to the right. And by the time he recovered his balance, Toby Downer was already scrambling to his feet.

Flyn had to act quickly. If he could dodge past Toby Downer, he was in the clear. Flyn clenched his fists, steeling himself. It was now or never. Ready. Set . . .

Then the Dimble brothers arrived, puffing and panting to cut him off.

He was too late.

'Where you going to run now, chicken?' Toby Downer sneered, rubbing his bleeding palms against his shorts.

Flyn could see the cycle path over Toby Downer's shoulder. If he wasn't a chicken, he'd charge at all three of them. That would surprise them! But he *was* a chicken, just like Toby Downer said.

Flyn slowly backed away up the hill instead. But he couldn't go far. The track to Lookout Hill was closed. A red barrier was strung between two bright red signs—*DANGER! KEEP OUT! MUDSLIDES!*

'Get him!' Toby Downer snarled.

Without thinking, Flyn ducked under the barrier and ran.

The track climbed steeply. Flyn's heart pounded and his lungs felt like they were going to explode. But he didn't slow down. Every time he heard a snapping branch, he imagined it was one of Toby Downer's gang catching up to him.

At least he was heading towards school. He'd used this track all the time before it was closed. It was a longer walk, but he didn't have to go past Toby Downer's house if he came this way. Once he was at the top of Lookout Hill, he could take another track downhill to Johnson's Field, which wasn't far from school. If he hurried, he might still make it to school on time . . .

Flyn rounded a corner and suddenly jerked to a halt.

Whoever had put up the warning signs was right about the mudslides! The track disappeared beneath a muddy wreckage of roots and sprawling, snapped tree trunks.
Flyn forgot all about being on time. He'd be happy if he made it to school at all!

Two

On the other side of the valley,
Pop Hooper's truck slowly wound its
way up Craggy Hill Road. The road
was curvy, so Pop gripped the steering
wheel tightly, trying to take each
corner smoothly. He didn't want the
animals getting motion sickness.

'Slowcoach!' Marshmallow, the
cockatoo, squawked from the

passenger seat. His crest stood to
attention while his head bobbed up
and down. Marshmallow loved
driving fast.

'You can always get out and fly,
you know.' Pop gave Marshmallow's
belly a friendly poke. 'You could do
with some exercise.'

When they reached the top, Pop
braked to a halt. Directly below, the

town was coming to life. The town square filled with market stalls and the sound of children drifted up from the school playground.

Pop hardly noticed. His eyes followed an invisible path through the park, over the river, then up Lookout Hill on the opposite side of the valley. Pop could just make out the track curling towards the top.

When he reached an ugly gash of mud and uprooted trees, his eyes narrowed. A small figure stood on the edge of the mudslide. After a moment, Pop chuckled. 'Looks like we made it just in time.'

The road began to tremble as the truck picked up speed.

Three

Flyn stood on the edge of the
mudslide. He had to keep going.
He couldn't stay there—another
mudslide could happen any second.
And he couldn't turn back. Toby
Downer's gang might be hiding
anywhere.

The earth and stones on the
surface of the mudslide looked loose.

They could start sliding again at the slightest touch. Flyn took a deep breath, then gently placed one foot on top. The surface felt solid enough. He leant forward. His foot slipped on the loose earth. Little rocks tumbled down the steep hill.

Flyn yanked his foot away just in time. His tongue felt like sandpaper. Maybe if he promised to do all Toby Downer's assignments for the year . . .

Then he sighed and began scrambling across the mudslide as fast as he could. Rocks and dirt slid away from under him, and he almost went tumbling headfirst down the hill, but he kept moving forward and just managed to keep his balance.

As he scrambled across, Flyn
aimed for objects which looked solid.
He leapt onto a root clump, tiptoed
across a wobbly branch, then sprang
to a big rock. His knees trembled and
his stomach knotted with fear.
He could set off another mudslide
at any time! But he didn't pause.
He flung himself forward again and

again, bounding from rock to tree stump to fence post. It was like playing hopscotch in a minefield.

Finally, Flyn landed on solid ground on the other side of the mudslide. He was shaking all over. But it wasn't safe to rest there. Flyn ran on.

*

On top of Lookout Hill was a coin-operated telescope. Flyn used to look through it on the way to school to see where Toby's gang was hanging out.

Flyn didn't have any money today, but as he paused to catch his breath, he still peeked into the telescope. He was astounded when the town square leapt into focus down below.

He nervously swung the telescope back the way he'd come, half-expecting to see Toby Downer gasping up the hill. But the track was empty. He followed the river to the school, then zoomed in on the playground. But he couldn't find Toby Downer's gang anywhere.

Suddenly the telescope spun left, then right. Then it slowly tilted towards the top of Craggy Hill on the opposite side of the valley, as if drawn by a giant magnet. Flyn had to bend down to look through the eyepiece.

He twiddled the focus knob . . .

His mouth gaped open. The longest, shiniest truck he'd ever seen was winding down Craggy Hill Road. The words written on the side of each wagon in gold letters made his heart beat faster: *Pop Hooper's Pet Express. Perfect Pets Guaranteed!*

Flyn knew *exactly* what sort of pet he wanted. A dog. Not just any dog, but the biggest, fiercest dog ever.

A dog that was afraid of nothing.
Then Flyn wouldn't feel so scared of
everything because Chomper (that's
what he'd call him) would be there to
protect him. And if the promise on
the truck was true, it wouldn't be Flyn
getting chased across mudslides next
time. It would be Toby Downer.

Four

Flyn crashed through the forest like an elephant. Branches whipped his face and brambles snagged his socks. But he kept running.

He had to catch that truck.

At the bottom of the hill the track turned right, curving around a big clearing in the forest called Johnson's Field.

From there he could sprint to Johnson's Bridge, and then run back across the river to wave down the truck on the main road.

But Flyn suddenly didn't have the strength to run another step. It was over a kilometre from Johnson's Bridge to Craggy Hill Road. He'd never make it in time.

As he came to a stop, panting, he thought he heard barking. He held his breath and listened hard. He *could* hear barking. And yapping and squeaking and squawking too! The sounds were coming from Johnson's Field.

Flyn knew he should be racing to school. Mrs Nostil was going to be furious. But he'd already made up his mind. He stumbled down the bank, burst into the clearing ... then stopped dead.

A long, shiny truck stretched right across Johnson's Field. It looked like the truck he'd seen crawling down Craggy Hill Road minutes before. But that was impossible!

The animal noises grew louder as Flyn crept closer. It sounded more like a circus than a pet shop. Hopefully there would be no clowns. Flyn was scared of clowns.

'SQUAWK!'

Flyn caught a glimpse of something white swooping towards him from the sky. He didn't know what it was, so he took no chances.

He dropped to the ground and
covered his face with his hands.

A moment later, something heavy
landed on Flyn's head. It didn't hurt
him, but Flyn was too scared to move.

Then he heard a friendly chuckle.

Flyn slowly lifted his head and
peeked through his fingers. At first he
thought he was seeing things.

A strange-looking man was walking *upside down* in front of him, with a pair of silver shoes on his hands. The man's silver suit sparkled like diamonds, and his curly silver moustache drooped over his silver eyes.

Suddenly an enormous upside down head leant down to block Flyn's view. It had white feathers, a black beak, and beady eyes which were staring right at him. Flyn's fingers snapped shut and he scrunched his eyes closed again.

'You'll be pleased to know cockatoos are vegetarians,' the strange man said. 'So unless your head's made of cabbage, you've got nothing to worry about.'

Flyn slowly opened his eyes. But as he took his hands away, the cockatoo on his head squawked 'Cabbage head!' in his ear. Then it nipped Flyn's nose. When Flyn yelped, it fluttered to the ground.

'Welcome to Pop Hooper's Pet Express!' the man cried as Flyn rubbed his nose. 'I'm Pop Hooper. And that is Marshmallow.'

The cockatoo did a headstand. It looked very pleased with itself.

Mister Hooper backflipped onto his feet. He shook his shoes from his hands, then held a hand out to Flyn.

'It's a scary business finding your perfect pet, Flyn,' Mister Hooper said.

'So, well done for being brave enough
to take the first step.'

Flyn gulped. Mister Hooper must
be thinking of somebody else. Flyn
wasn't brave *at all*. If he was brave,
he wouldn't run away from Toby
Downer's gang. He'd stand up to
them, just like his dad said he
should. But he thanked Mister
Hooper anyway.

'Great!' Mister Hooper said. 'One perfect pet coming right up.' He bent closer and winked. 'It's guaranteed, you know.'

Before Flyn could say a word, Mister Hooper cartwheeled along the line of wagons, disappearing behind the last one.

Flyn watched, open-mouthed.

'Chop chop!' Marshmallow squawked, flying off.

Flyn struggled to his feet, too confused to follow right away. How did Mister Hooper know his name? And how did he know Flyn wanted a pet? Even Flyn's dad didn't know that.

Five

By the time Flyn reached the other side of the long row of wagons, there was no sign of Mister Hooper or Marshmallow. But Flyn wasn't alone. The field swarmed with every kind of pet imaginable.

Everywhere Flyn looked, lemurs spun cartwheels, and hares sprinted zigzags in the long grass. Rabbits

dug burrows and an aardvark sniffed
for ants. Flyn saw guinea pigs and
possums, cats and squirrels. A family
of meerkats stood to attention while
a grumpy wombat waddled past.
Nearly all the animals were fluffy
and seemed harmless. Still, Flyn
was relieved when Mister Hooper
reappeared.

'So, Flyn,' Mister Hooper said, 'let's hear about this perfect pet of yours.'

Flyn opened his mouth, but no words came out. It was one thing to dream about your perfect pet, and another thing to tell a stranger about it. Flyn didn't even like talking in front of his class. His face flushed red.

'Why don't you start by telling me his name?' said Mister Hooper.

'His name's Chomper,' Flyn said, glancing sideways at Mister Hooper. He'd probably think that was a stupid name.

But Mister Hooper nodded as if it was a good name. 'What sort of animal is Chomper?' he asked.

'He's a dog,' said Flyn.

'A dog, eh? Good choice,' Mister Hooper said. 'And I bet he's fierce, too, with a name like Chomper.'

'He's the fiercest dog in the world,' Flyn agreed.

As he started talking about Chomper, Flyn forgot about being nervous.

He described how, when Chomper barked, it sounded like he was coughing, and how his left ear was floppier than the right one. Then he listed all the things Chomper wasn't afraid of—like snakes and darkness and clowns and caterpillars—which happened to be exactly the same things Flyn *was* afraid of. So it was a very long list.

Flyn even told Mister Hooper about how Toby Downer's gang wouldn't dare steal Flyn's lunch or copy his homework once Flyn had Chomper.

When Flyn finally ran out of things to say, Mister Hooper scratched his chin. '*Hmmm.* I don't have any dogs like that with me today. They're too much trouble to bring in the truck. Always getting into fights and trying to prove how tough they are.'

Flyn sighed. He knew getting his perfect pet couldn't be *that* easy.

Mister Hooper chuckled. 'Don't look so glum, Flyn. I guaranteed you a perfect pet, so a perfect pet you shall have. Now sit down for a moment. I'll be right back.'

Flyn flopped to the ground.
I probably don't even deserve a dog like Chomper, he thought. *Mister Hooper promised a perfect pet, but he probably meant a chicken. A chicken would be perfect for me. That's what Toby Downer would say. But maybe Mister Hooper will let me have Chomper anyway.*

Flyn was so busy thinking, he didn't hear tiny footsteps scurrying towards him. Suddenly something fat and scruffy jumped onto his lap and began licking his face.

'*Urrrgggghhh!*' Flyn held his arms out for protection. But it was no use. The dog was so round and solid, once its head squirmed through a gap, Flyn couldn't stop the rest of it from following, no matter how tightly he squeezed his arms together. Each time the dog licked Flyn's face, it yapped with excitement.

'Ha! Pumpkin likes you! I knew he would.' Mister Hooper scooped the dog up in his arms. 'That's a good start.'

Pumpkin yapped and tried to
break free of Mister Hooper's grasp.

Flyn's bottom lip started to
tremble. If this was a joke . . .

'I'm not making fun of you, Flyn,'
Mister Hooper said kindly. 'But
controlling a dog like Chomper will
take courage. So it's a good idea to
start you with something smaller.

If you can control Pumpkin for one night, I guarantee you'll have your perfect pet by the morning. Deal?'

When Flyn nodded, Mister Hooper said: 'Let's shake on it'.

Flyn held out his hand. But Mister Hooper held out Pumpkin's paw instead. Flyn felt silly shaking the dog's paw, but Pumpkin yapped with delight.

'Right, then. I'll see you both tomorrow.' Mister Hooper gave Flyn a wink. Then he gave Pumpkin a bigger one.

Six

Flyn was dreading facing Mrs Nostil. Being late for school was bad enough, and now he had to find a way to hide Pumpkin, too! But he was determined to get it over with. In fact, he couldn't wait for the day to end. Tomorrow he'd get Chomper, and then Toby Downer's gang would never bother him again.

Still, today was going to be tough. As he hurried along the track, Flyn kept imagining what Toby Downer would say if he saw Flyn with Pumpkin. The whole school would laugh at him!

The track turned right, and Johnson's Bridge loomed ahead. Flyn shivered. It was the perfect place for another ambush. Even though it looked deserted, and Flyn could see traffic whizzing along the main road on the other side, his mouth felt like it was full of cottonwool.

Don't be ridiculous, Flyn told himself. *Even Toby Downer wouldn't be this late for school just to get me back.*

Flyn glanced over his shoulder.

Surely Pumpkin would know if Toby Downer was hiding nearby? He might not be Chomper, but he was still a dog, and should sense danger. But Pumpkin was trailing ten metres behind. He seemed to be daydreaming. His tongue was hanging so low, it nearly brushed the ground.

Flyn waited impatiently for Pumpkin to catch up. When Pumpkin ran right into the back of Flyn's legs, Flyn realised Pumpkin was no help at all. Flyn was on his own, and would have to make a run for it.

Flyn took a deep breath. 'Ready, Pumpkin?'

The pigeons resting on the bridge

wheeled into the sky as Flyn rumbled
past. When he made it to the
footpath on the other side, he
cheered. There was nobody there!

'We made it, Pumpkin,' he said.

But Pumpkin was still standing at
the far end of the bridge.

'Pumpkin! Hurry up!' Flyn called.

Pumpkin didn't move.

'Hurry up! I'll leave you behind!'
Flyn said, although he didn't mean it.
Mister Hooper would never give him
Chomper if he left Pumpkin behind.

But Flyn didn't want to recross the

bridge. He glanced nervously along the main road. There was no sign of Toby Downer's gang. But they could turn up at any second.

Then the sound of whimpering drifted across the river. Flyn hurried back over the bridge. 'I haven't got time for games,' he grumbled. But Pumpkin wasn't playing, he was trembling like a water balloon in an earthquake.

At first Flyn couldn't see what had scared Pumpkin.

Then a pigeon fluttered to the
ground nearby and Pumpkin nearly
did a backflip.

Flyn bent down and scratched
Pumpkin behind the ears. He wasn't
angry any more. 'It's OK, Pumpkin.
The pigeons won't hurt you. Come
on.' Flyn slowly backed over the
bridge, urging Pumpkin along.
'Good boy. That's it. Keep going.'

Pumpkin followed Flyn, but every
time a pigeon came close, he flinched.
Reaching the other side took forever.

As Flyn stepped backwards onto

the footpath, he felt a hand on his shoulder. His heart sank.

'Watch where you're going!' a voice said.

But it wasn't Toby Downer, it was just a stranger hurrying past. Yet, Flyn didn't feel relieved. He felt angry with himself. What if it *had been* Toby Downer? Flyn would have walked right into an ambush!

Soon, Pumpkin joined Flyn on the footpath, His tail wagged and he stood up against Flyn's leg and licked Flyn's hand. But Flyn hardly noticed.

As they waited to cross the main road, Flyn's eyes patrolled the street. He wouldn't be caught off guard again.

*

Across the road was Mister Glasden's house. He was the school caretaker. The school was tucked in behind, down a narrow street.

'Not far now,' Flyn said to Pumpkin.

As they reached Mister Glasden's yard, they heard a menacing growl. Suddenly, Mister Glasden's dog, Devil, stood up against the high, wooden fence and started barking ferociously. Even though it happened every day, and Flyn knew Devil couldn't reach him, it still frightened him. He broke into a sprint.

Flyn raced along the footpath with Devil following on the other side of the fence. When Flyn reached the corner, he hooked one hand around the end of the fence and catapulted himself down the footpath towards the school gates.

Flyn was panting like a marathon runner by the time he reached the end of Mister Glasden's yard. He expected Pumpkin to be behind him. But he should have known better.

Why aren't I surprised? Flyn thought, when he heard Pumpkin whimpering in the distance. *I'll never get Chomper at this rate!*

Then Flyn took a deep breath.
'I'm coming, Pumpkin!' he yelled.
Doing his best to ignore Devil, Flyn
took the corner so sharply, his feet
nearly slipped out from beneath him.
Pumpkin was still outside the far end
of Mister Glasden's yard.

As Flyn came panting to a halt,
he noticed Grabby, the school cat,
perched in a tree in the corner of
Mister Glasden's yard, looking down
at Pumpkin with interest. When
Grabby saw Flyn, he sprang down
to the footpath.

Pumpkin started backing away,
whimpering.

'It's OK. I'm here now, Pumpkin,'
Flyn said softly.

Pumpkin was relieved to see Flyn. He forgot all about the cat and scampered forwards, yapping with excitement. Grabby arched his back and hissed loudly. Pumpkin froze in astonishment. Then, before Flyn could react, Pumpkin spun round and fled back down the street. He was heading away from the school as fast as his stumpy legs could carry him!

Groaning, Flyn set off in pursuit.

Seven

Flyn expected Pumpkin to head back
to Johnson's Field. But when Pumpkin
reached the corner, he turned right
instead.

Flyn winced. The old rubbish tip
behind the school was out of bounds.
If anyone saw him there, he'd be
expelled.

But he couldn't let Pumpkin go

into the tip alone. Pumpkin was so small, he could get stuck in a drain, or fall down a rabbit hole. Or get attacked by rats. Or eat something poisonous. Or . . .

'Pumpkin!' Flyn's pace quickened as the possibilities ran through his mind. He'd never get Chomper if he couldn't even look after Pumpkin!

Pumpkin squeezed through the gate at the old tip and his barking reached a crescendo. Flyn struggled to catch up. The tip had been closed years ago, but some people kept dumping their rubbish there. It stank, and plastic bags lay all over the muddy ground. A flock of crows circled above, cawing with annoyance.

Flyn clambered through a hole in the gate and looked around. At the far end of the tip was a steep clay bank. Pumpkin was scampering back and forward along the top, barking at every crow's shadow. Suddenly a crow swooped down to land on the bank. Pumpkin jumped sideways ... and disappeared.

'Pumpkin!' Flyn's feet were moving before he had time to think.

'*YAP! YAP! YAP!*' Pumpkin answered.

Flyn dragged himself, slipping and sliding, up the bank. 'I'm coming, Pumpkin!'

But when he reached the top, he realised he was in trouble. Directly

below was a pool of stagnant water,
the surface thick with algae. In the
middle, struggling to stay afloat, was
Pumpkin. Only his head was above
water, and it was covered in slime.

Pumpkin churned the water into
foam with his paws and scrabbled
at the bank, desperately trying to
climb back up the way he'd fallen in.

But the steep bank was too slippery.

'Swim the other way!' Flyn waved his arms, trying to shoo Pumpkin in the opposite direction. 'It's less steep on the other side!'

But Flyn waved his arms too hard, and his feet slipped out from beneath him. He clutched at the bank, but couldn't get a grip. He slid down the bank like an avalanche, terrified of the deep water, and what people had dumped in it. There could be broken glass, or rusty wire! Or his feet could get stuck in the muddy bottom, and then . . .

Flyn hit the water with a splash. Mud and slime washed over him. He didn't know which way was up or

down, but he kept thrashing until he
burst to the surface, gasping for air.
His mouth was filled with foul-tasting
water. Algae clotted his nose. He
almost screamed when he felt
something wrap around his ankle.
But he kicked out again and his
feet found the bottom. He stood up.
The water was only up to his knees.

Flyn suddenly laughed.

It's not as dangerous as it looks, he thought.

. . . unless you were a small dog like Pumpkin and *couldn't swim*!

Pumpkin was spinning in furious circles, barely keeping afloat. His snout was covered by a soggy tissue. Each time he lifted a paw and tried to wipe it off, his head sank underwater.

Flyn floundered forward and scooped Pumpkin into his arms. 'You're safe now,' he cried, peeling the tissue off Pumpkin's nose.

As Flyn waded across the pond, he didn't think once about all the nasty things lying on the bottom. He was too busy cleaning Pumpkin's face.

And Pumpkin was busy licking mud off Flyn's arm.

But as they climbed the bank, Flyn spotted the school. His fears flooded back. He was already late, and now he was wet and smelly to boot!

I'll have to hide Pumpkin in the store cupboard, he thought.

It was going to be a long day. Flyn hoped getting Chomper would be worth it.

'Come on, Pumpkin,' he said wearily.

Eight

Flyn was right. Mrs Nostil wasn't pleased when he arrived at school late, soaking wet *and* covered in slime.

'Would you care to share your adventures with the class, Mister Fletcher?' she said

Toby Downer snorted loudly.

Flyn looked nervously around the room, licking his lips.

'Well?' asked Mrs Nostil.

Toby Downer smirked. Flyn's face flushed red. Flyn felt himself getting tongue-tied.

Suddenly the door swung open and Pumpkin burst into the room. Flyn had hidden Pumpkin in the store cupboard as planned, but he hadn't been able to shut the door completely.

Pumpkin must have wriggled out somehow. Now he was racing under the desks, sniffing at everyone's feet. The class giggled and shouted. Mrs Nostil grabbed her ruler.

'Shoo, you filthy creature!' she cried, storming towards Pumpkin.

Flyn jumped up. 'Don't hurt him!'

The whole class held their breath as Mrs Nostil gave Flyn her iciest stare. 'You'd better have a jolly good explanation,' she said.

Suddenly Flyn found his voice. He told the class everything ... well, *almost* everything. He didn't mention Mister Hooper in case *everyone* wanted a perfect pet. Instead, he told them he'd found Pumpkin alone at

Johnson's Field. But the rest was true.

The whole class listened quietly to Flyn's story. Only Toby Downer fiddled with his pen and pretended to be bored. 'What a lame story,' he sneered.

Flyn was very surprised when Jason Dimble went: *'Shhhhh!'*

'That's the best excuse for being late I've heard in a long while,' said Mrs Nostil. She sounded almost amused. 'I hope you were taking notes, Mister Downer. You could do with a few excuses like that.'

Toby Downer blushed.

'I do have one question though,' Mrs Nostil went on. 'What were you doing in Johnson's Field?'

Flyn looked at Toby Downer. When
Toby Downer started wriggling in his
seat, Flyn smiled. 'I was doing
research for a nature project,' he
fibbed.

Mrs Nostil smiled too. 'Go and put
on some dry clothes before you get
cold. Then I think your classmates
have a few questions for you.'

*

Some of Flyn's classmates called
him a hero. But he didn't feel like a
hero. Heroes were supposed to be
brave. When Flyn fell in the dam,
he'd been as scared as Pumpkin.
But he'd had to do *something*.
Pumpkin needed him. And it wasn't
brave to walk across a mudslide,
either. It was stupid. Mudslides
were far more dangerous than
Toby Downer. But once Flyn had
Chomper, he wouldn't worry about
mudslides, or dams, or Toby Downer
any more.

At lunchtime Flyn joined in a
game of soccer. Every time the ball
was kicked out, Pumpkin sped after it.

But when he tried to stop it, he got bowled over. Flyn's classmates thought it was so funny, they started kicking the ball out on purpose, just to watch Pumpkin go tumbling.

Only Toby Downer was unamused. He was the best player in the school and always showed off. But he couldn't show off without an audience. So once he had the ball, he kicked it as hard as he could. The ball went sailing over the fence— right into Mister Glasden's yard.

'Nice one, Downer,' Conor Tobin, the school captain, grumbled. 'You'd better fetch it, or I'll tell Mrs Nostil.'

'Why don't you ask Mrs *Nostril* to fetch it?' said Toby Downer. He turned to the Dimble brothers, but they looked away, embarrassed.

'Fetch the ball,' Conor repeated, as everyone else nodded in agreement.

'It's not my ball,' Toby Downer said. He was acting cool, but his face was red. Then he smiled nastily. 'Look, the stupid mutt is getting your ball. If Devil doesn't get him first.'

Flyn spun round to see Pumpkin wriggling under the fence. 'No!' he yelled. Not giving a thought to splinters or nails, Flyn leapt onto the fence, hooked his fingers over the boards, and hoisted himself until his head poked over the top.

Pumpkin was yapping excitedly and wrestling with the ball.

'*Shhhh*, Pumpkin,' Flyn whispered.

'Come here, boy! Come on!'

There was no sign of Devil. Yet.

Pumpkin wasn't leaving without

the ball. He leapt at it, trying to

nudge it back towards the fence.

But his paws slipped off and he went

somersaulting over the top.

'Leave the stupid ball!' Flyn hissed.

Devil could appear at any second.

Pumpkin lunged at the ball again. It flew in the air then started bouncing towards the house. Pumpkin chased it, yapping loudly.

Flyn heaved himself over the fence and tumbled into Mister Glasden's yard. Pumpkin jumped up in greeting as if his legs were springs.

Flyn flicked the ball towards the fence, then scooped Pumpkin up. He carefully backed away. At the first sign of Devil, he was going to run ...

A low, throaty growl rumbled across the yard. Flyn's face turned white. It was too late to run. Devil crept out of the shadows beside Mister Glasden's shed.

Flyn tried to tell himself he wasn't afraid. But his heart was pounding loudly. Everything else sounded *very* far away.

Without taking his eyes off Devil, Flyn crouched down and pushed Pumpkin back under the fence. 'Go on, boy. You're safe now.'

Devil stalked closer, still growling.

Flyn glanced over his shoulder. Fearful eyes peered through every crack in the fence. Two boys from his class were hanging over the top, holding out their hands. They looked very far away. Flyn knew he'd never make it. But he had to try. Every muscle tingled as he got ready to jump. On the count of three. One, two—

Flyn groaned as Pumpkin burst back through the gap, his tiny teeth bared and his scruffy fur standing on end.

Devil snarled. The muscles on his back rippled with anger.

Flyn's legs trembled. But he stood his ground. 'Get! Scram!' he yelled. Pumpkin stood beside him, snarling like a wind-up propeller.

Devil looked from one to the other as if deciding who to chew first.

Suddenly, Flyn's foot shot out and sent the ball looping towards Devil. Devil lunged sideways, snatching it out of midair. The ball burst as his fangs snapped shut.

This took all the time Flyn and Pumpkin needed. Pumpkin shot through the gap, while Flyn scrambled up the fence. His friends'

hands hauled him upwards. He just managed to pull his legs out of the way before Devil slammed against the fence, snarling with rage.

Safe on the other side, Flyn collapsed, panting, on the ground.

Pumpkin jumped all over him. 'You're the bravest dog ever!' Flyn laughed. 'Who needs a Chomper when I've got you!'

Toby Downer jumped down from the fence, shaking his head disgustedly. He opened his mouth, but nobody was listening. The Dimble brothers crowded around with everyone else, jostling to be the first to pat Flyn on the back.

Nine

When Flyn got home from school,
he made sandwiches for himself and
Pumpkin, and then took Pumpkin
into the back yard.

They played fetch and tag and
hide-and-seek. Pumpkin was so full of
energy, Flyn could hardly keep up.
When Flyn stopped to catch his breath,
Pumpkin raced round like a tornado.

They were in the middle of a game
of tug of war when Flyn's dad
came home.

Pumpkin sprinted across the yard
and flipped onto his back. Waving
his legs in the air like an overturned
beetle, he wriggled and squirmed
against Flyn's dad's shoes, yapping
with excitement.

'What a reception!' Flyn's dad bent down and stroked Pumpkin's belly. 'You're a cute wee fellow, aren't you?'

'His name's Pumpkin,' Flyn said.

'Funny name.' His dad smiled. 'Whose dog is it?'

Flyn started to say Pumpkin was *his* dog, but he suddenly realised he couldn't say that *at all*. Even if his dad said he could keep Pumpkin, Mister Hooper certainly hadn't given him permission to do so!

Flyn sighed. 'I'm looking after him tonight. But I have to give him back in the morning.'

'That's a shame,' his dad said. 'You two get along well. And it'd be nice to have a dog around the house.'

Flyn nodded sadly. 'I'm going to miss him.'

Flyn's dad squeezed his shoulder. 'I'm sure his owner misses him just as much.'

'But he's not *really* Pumpkin's owner,' Flyn grumbled. 'And he's got loads of animals already. He probably wouldn't even notice Pumpkin was gone!'

'Maybe you should ask if you can keep Pumpkin then.'

Flyn's dad was getting confused. So Flyn nodded, even though he knew Mister Hooper would never let him keep Pumpkin. Flyn was supposed to have looked after Pumpkin, but instead Pumpkin had rescued *him*!

Flyn knew he didn't deserve Pumpkin. He didn't deserve *any* dog. But it was nice having him around.

That night Flyn slept like a log, with Pumpkin curled up at his feet. Pumpkin might not be as fearless as Chomper, but that didn't matter. Friends didn't have to be brave all the time. But when you really needed them, friends were there for you. Flyn tried not to think about the morning, when he would have to say goodbye to his new friend.

*

Flyn was in no hurry to get to Johnson's Field the next morning. He loitered at every corner, happy to wait while Pumpkin sniffed around.

Every few paces he paused to scratch
Pumpkin behind his ears. He wished
he could make time stop, so he
wouldn't have to say goodbye.

All the way, Flyn told himself that
Pumpkin would be better off without
him. He'd be so happy to be going
home, he wouldn't even notice when
Flyn left. Flyn was just feeling sorry
for himself, that was all.

But when Flyn saw the forest
opening up ahead, he ached to turn
around and flee back home.

Then he took a deep breath and
kept walking. A deal was a deal.
Mister Hooper had promised Flyn his
perfect pet, and Flyn had promised to
return Pumpkin. What a stupid deal!

Pumpkin *was* perfect. Flyn sighed. He couldn't even look after a perfect dog.

Pumpkin strutted ahead. He seemed keen to get there.

At the edge of Johnson's Field, Flyn jerked to a halt. For a few seconds, he couldn't move. He couldn't even think. All he could do was stand there like a dummy, blinking in disbelief.

Johnson's Field was empty.

Mister Hooper was gone.

'Mister Hooper!' Flyn walked around the field, calling loudly. There was no answer. There were no tyre-marks or animal footprints, either. In fact, there was no sign that the truck had ever been there. He circled the field twice, scratching his head.

Suddenly, Pumpkin
started barking and
ran off into the grass.

'Wait for me!'
Flyn called. He ran
after Pumpkin,
following the trail
weaving through
the long grass.
He caught up as
Pumpkin reached
the forest. 'What is it,
boy?' he asked.

For an answer,
Pumpkin
sprang up
against
a tree.

Pinned to the trunk was a note, addressed to Flyn:

Dear Flyn,

Remember I said you had to be brave to own a dog like Chomper? Well, that's true. But what I didn't say was you have to be even braver to own a dog like Pumpkin. Chompers just need discipline. And discipline is easy. But Pumpkin needs lots more than that. Lucky for Pumpkin, I think you might be brave enough to give him everything he needs. Good Luck! Pop Hooper

For a few seconds, Flyn just stood there, blinking. Then he started to run. Pumpkin wasn't far behind.

Halfway across the field, Flyn tripped over a rock and sprawled forward into the long grass. He was surprised when he didn't get hurt at all. Shaking his head, he rolled onto his back. Pumpkin leapt onto his chest.

As Flyn gazed up into the clear, blue sky, a smile spread across his face. Then he started to laugh.

Ten

On Craggy Hill Road, a flicker of
silver danced in the sun.

Pop Hooper knew Flyn couldn't
see him, but he waved anyway, until
Flyn disappeared into the forest. He
wished he could have said goodbye
properly, but he was afraid Flyn might
be *too* brave. Brave enough to keep
his promise to return Pumpkin.

Even though that was the last thing
either of them wanted.

Pop couldn't risk that.

'ZOOM! ZOOM!' Marshmallow
squawked. He leant out the cabin
window and attacked his reflection in
the wing mirror.

'If you're not careful I'm going to
make Warren my co-driver,' Pop
chuckled as he climbed up into the
driver's seat.

'Co-toad! Co-toad!' Marshmallow shook his head.

'Yeah, I guess I'm stuck with you. Warren's got a terrible sense of direction.' Pop leant out the window and gazed upwards, as if the clouds

were words scratched on the sky that he could read. After a moment, he nodded. 'Right, then. Off we go!'

He turned the key and the engine roared into life.

About the Author

Kyle Mewburn lives in a house
with a roof made of grass, in the
middle of nowhere in the far south
of New Zealand's South Island.

Kyle once had a pet rooster called
Oscar. Oscar was more of a pecky
pet than a pesky pet. He'd peck
anything that looked like a worm,
even shoelaces! He used to perch on
Kyle's shoulder and peck Kyle's
eyelashes every time he blinked.
Luckily for Kyle, he was a good shot.

About the Artist

Heath McKenzie lives in Melbourne, Australia, in a slightly cracked and rotted weatherboard house which he loves. His favourite animals are elephants and bees. He thinks an elephant crossed with a bee would be the best animal ever.

Heath owns a little dog called Ed, who enjoys sneaking into bedrooms and then running around madly with any stray clothes he can find—preferably socks or underpants!

Other Titles in the Series

If only Lily could find her perfect kitten, she wouldn't be lonely any more. So when Pop Hooper gives her a smelly, scruffy cat to take care of for a night she is horrifed.

Surely everyone will laugh at her now ... won't they?

Available now!